In memory of David Hutchison,
who loved the grand metropolis.

Library of Congress info TK.

ISBN 0-8431-7677-6

A B C D E F G H I J

THE LITTLE SKYSCRAPER

Scott Santoro

PSS!

PRICE STERN SLOAN

The little skyscraper was not always so little. Many years ago, he was the tallest building in the city. He was covered in the finest limestone money could buy, and he had a shiny gold spire and fancy silver trim. At his base was a pretty little park.

GRAND

KING KONG

He was so tall that sometimes his head peeked above the clouds . . .

. . . and on sunny days he could cast a shadow over four blocks long!

Everyone looked up to the little skyscraper—especially a young boy named Jack. Jack would always ask his parents to stop and see the little skyscraper whenever they were visiting the city.

GRAND

THE FOUNTAINHEAD

Jack and his parents would ride the elevator up to the little skyscraper's observation deck. They weren't alone. People came from near and far to admire the sweeping view. Sometimes even the little skyscraper got dizzy from looking down.

"I want to be an architect when I grow up," Jack announced. His parents thought it was a wonderful idea. "You can do anything you put your mind to," his father encouraged. "Maybe someday you'll even work on a beautiful building like this one."

The little skyscraper beamed with pride.

As the years passed, the little skyscraper watched the city grow and change around him. Many of the older buildings were torn down . . .

WOLFE'S
DEPART

ON THIS
SITE
MODERN
OFFICE
TOWER!

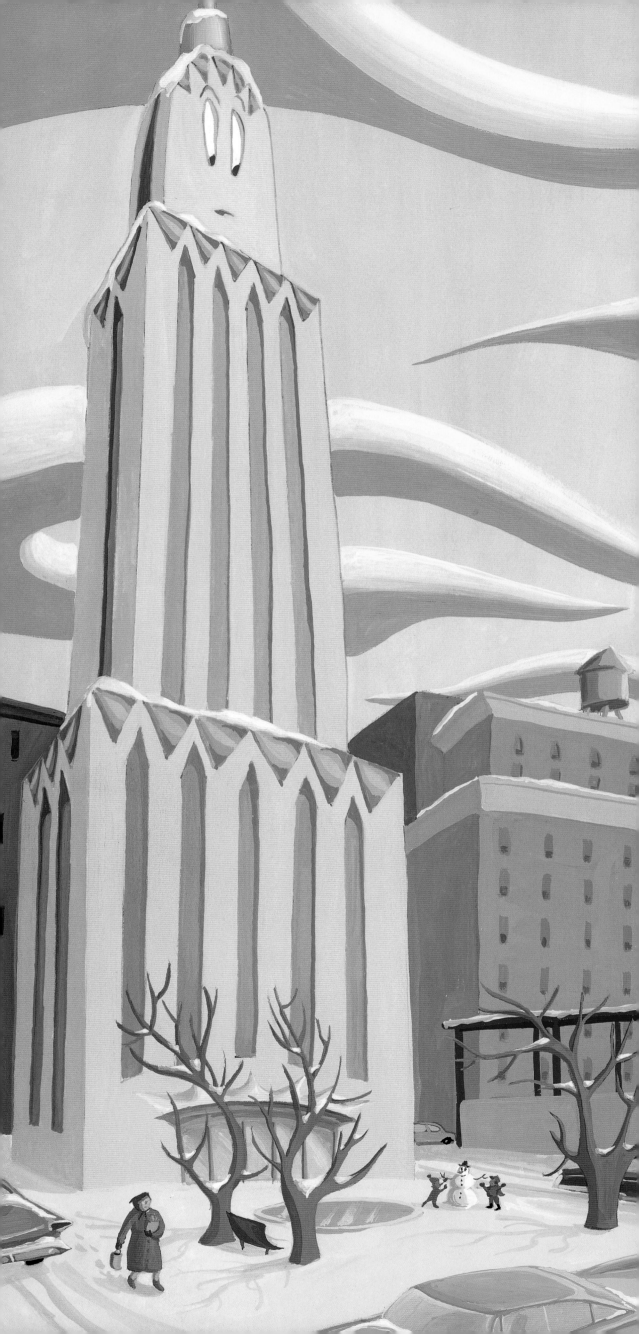

One day, the little skyscraper realized he was no longer the tallest building in the city. The pretty little park was turned into a parking lot.

And the city continued to grow.

The new buildings grew taller

and **taller**

and **taller**.

Which made the little
skyscraper feel smaller

and smaller

and smaller.

It appeared as if no one cared about the little skyscraper anymore. People seemed much more impressed with the sleek, new modern buildings made of glass and steel. He felt *very* old-fashioned. His limestone had become stained and dirty, and his shiny spire was now dull and tarnished.

One morning, he woke up to find a huge sign erected at his base. The little skyscraper was going to be torn down!

Nearby, a man on his way to work also saw the sign. It was Jack! Now grown up, he had indeed become an architect—all because of the little skyscraper!

37 CINEMAS

Jack decided that he had to do something. He soon found that many other people loved the little skyscraper too. They picketed and held rallies, and together they convinced the mayor to declare the little skyscraper a landmark—an honor that only the most special buildings achieve.

But that wasn't all! The mayor appointed Jack to oversee the little skyscraper's complete restoration. His limestone was cleaned and his gold spire and silver trim were polished.

And the pretty little park was replanted!

On the day the scaffolding came down, everyone, even the tallest, most modern buildings, looked up to the little skyscraper.